# EXTREME CAREERS™

# HOMELAND SECURITY OFFICERS

Jared Meyer

rosen publishing's
**rosen central**®

New York

*To my mother, for her noble efforts in both protecting and training me whenever she would and as best as she could*

Published in 2007 by The Rosen Publishing Group, Inc.
29 East 21st Street, New York, NY 10010

First Edition

**Library of Congress Cataloging-in-Publication Date**

Meyer, Jared.
Homeland security officers / Jared Meyer.—1st ed.
p. cm.—(Extreme careers)
Includes bibliographical references and index.
ISBN-13: 978-1-4042-0945-9
ISBN-10: 1-4042-0945-X (library binding)
1. Police—United States—Juvenile literature. 2. Law enforcement—United States—Juvenile literature. 3. Law enforcement—Vocational guidance—United States—Juvenile literature. I. Title. II. Series.
HV8138.M46 2007
363.28023'73—dc22

                                                2006009201

*Manufactured in the United States of America*

**On the cover:** A U.S. Coast Guard officer patrolling American waters.

# Contents

# Introduction

The Department of Homeland Security was created shortly after the terrorist attacks in New York, Pennsylvania, and Washington, D.C., on September 11, 2001. The department was set up with the hope of defending America and protecting its citizens and visitors from people looking to harm them.

Within the Department of Homeland Security are a variety of agencies that focus on specific goals that are designed to maintain a strong and secure country. Each of the agencies is run by its own leader. Those leaders work with teams of brave, talented, and qualified security professionals, as well as with the other agencies in the department.

The Department of Homeland Security is a massive organization. There are more than 87,000 governmental jurisdictions across America that are part of the homeland security team. Each of these jurisdictions is organized into an agency that works under the department. These agencies include the Federal Emergency Management Agency (FEMA), the Domestic Nuclear Detection Office, and the Directorate for Science and Technology, which develops scientific and technological tools to help protect America. This book will focus on the three most exciting agencies to work for: the U.S. Coast Guard, the U.S. Customs and Border Protection, and the U.S. Secret Service.

While many of the jobs within the Department of Homeland Security may not be exciting, there are a good number of careers that are very thrilling and challenging. These jobs demand a very specific type of person who can perform tasks that most people would call risky, dangerous, or even hazardous to one's health and/or safety. Homeland security officers are prepared for these unusual jobs and often unconventional lifestyles.

Most kids are asked by friends or teachers what they want to be when they grow up. Many have dreamed about what it would be like to do exhilarating

PROTECTI

The Department of Homeland Security was formed soon after the terrorist attacks on September 11, 2001. Many government officials agreed that such an organization would help the nation prevent, fight, and recover from terrorist acts.

work while contributing to the protection of millions of people and even the entire country. In the future, if you want to build an exciting, challenging, and satisfying career, the Department of Homeland Security provides numerous opportunities.

# Types of Homeland Security Officers

There are many types of homeland security officers and many different areas within the Department of Homeland Security. Given the large scope of employment opportunities within the department, this book will cover Coast Guard officers, customs agents, and Secret Service agents in detail. These three career areas have one important thing in common, which is that the men and women who are a part of the U.S. Coast Guard, U.S. Customs and Border Protection, and U.S. Secret Service all serve their country and protect and defend its citizens and their way of life.

## Coast Guard Officers

Of the three career options within the Department of Homeland Security covered in this book, the U.S.

Jumping out of huge helicopters, learning to use defensive weapons, and becoming certified as rescue swimmers are among the many exciting opportunities that Coast Guard officers enjoy.

Coast Guard may be the most familiar agency to most people. The Coast Guard's red and white helicopters and boats are often seen in and around major waterways. According to its Web site, the Coast Guard is responsible for guarding America's coasts, ports, and inland waterways and protecting people from harm in those bodies of water. Now, more than ever, the Coast Guard is also called upon to investigate the existence of drugs on boats at the borders of the country, too.

## Coast Guard Border Patrol

The brave members of the Coast Guard are sometimes the first people defending U.S. borders in the event of an incoming threat to the country. For example, Coast Guard officers are often the first line of defense against terrorists attempting to enter the United States. After New York City was attacked on September 11, 2001, the Coast Guard was on site protecting the city's waterways from possible additional attacks by terrorists. Unfortunately, little could be done on its part to prevent the collapse of the

The border patrol team protects American citizens from terrorist attacks, especially in prime targets such as downtown Manhattan.

World Trade Center. The Coast Guard is also responsible for stopping illegal immigrants, people who are not registered to live in America, from successfully penetrating our borders.

# Coast Guard Search and Rescue

During the winter months in San Diego, whale watching is a popular pastime given that migrating whales appear most often during this time of the year. Imagine that people were visiting the city and that they decided to go on a whale-watching cruise, but halfway through the tour, the boat stopped working unexpectedly. The passengers would be stuck out in the Pacific Ocean with nowhere to go. While the cruise company's headquarters would likely be contacted, the Coast Guard could also be called to check in on the malfunctioning vessel and to see if anyone had any immediate needs just in case the cruise company's rescue ship didn't show up for a while.

# Drug Enforcement

If the Coast Guard finds a boat or ship that its team members feel is a threat to the safety and well-being of American citizens, it could request permission to board it and search for drugs or other potentially dangerous or illegal substances. Should something illegal be found, Coast Guard officers can make arrangements to prevent the ship's passengers from passing through American borders.

Like other authorities such as local police departments, the Coast Guard uses highly trained dogs to search for illegal substances. These animals can be very helpful in finding smuggled narcotics on boats.

One example of the many possible, uncertain scenarios that Coast Guard team members may face while protecting the country from dangerous and harmful substances could take place right off any American coast. On the Pacific Ocean one warm summer day, the Coast Guard team might receive word about a suspicious ship that was sighted off the coast of San Francisco. One of the organization's leaders would request that the ship be confronted.

If this were at night, it would be hard to see without powerful lights or night-vision goggles, which could make the task very dangerous. If the team members are unable to quickly and easily see if the suspects are concealing weapons, let alone illegal substances they are trying to import into the United States, the situation could be outright risky. This is why the Coast Guard is vital to the protection of American borders.

# Customs Agents

The U.S. Customs and Border Protection, which is a branch of the Department of Homeland Security, is an interesting agency to consider working for because

Sometimes, homeland security teams such as the U.S. Customs Service and the U.S. Coast Guard work together in stopping illegal drugs from crossing America's borders.

part of its responsibilities involves generating revenue that aids in the development of the United States infrastructure, like roads and defense. The U.S. government can be thought of as a very large business. In order to grow into a stronger and more effective organization, it needs money or revenue. The country generates revenue by requiring that taxes be paid on imported goods. Money has been earned for the development of the country for over 200 years thanks to the team members within the U.S. Customs Agency who monitor the goods that enter its borders.

There are three types of customs officers: customs service inspectors, who can be seen at airports checking in travelers from other countries; customs officers, who use trained dogs to find illegal drugs and dangerous explosives; and customs service agents, who have the most dangerous job in the agency.

Customs service agents attempt to prevent illegal and unwanted substances from entering the United States. They have one of the most important jobs in the Department of Homeland Security. Customs service agents protect us by land, by sea, and by air. Some customs agents investigate people whom they suspect are connected with crimes such as the importing of illegal drugs. Controlling the import and export of illegal drugs is one concern of customs agents, and as years go by, customs agents are keeping their eyes open for the illegal import of weapons that could potentially harm U.S. citizens.

Imagine for a moment that you are a customs service agent and you just spotted a suspicious-looking person placing a large package covered in brown paper underneath an airport bench. What would you do? You could call for backup just in case it is a package of active explosives, or you could run over to evaluate the situation personally to prevent a possible catastrophe from occurring. Maybe it's an abandoned package of narcotics — you just can't know. What if you hear a ticking sound coming from the package? Would you run away from it, or grab it and take it with you to an unoccupied location?

On the other hand, you could go after the person who placed the strange object underneath the bench, potentially preventing that person from doing additional harm in the near future. Now, imagine that the package was simply a gift for a loved one. Customs service agents often face these unexpected false alarms throughout their careers.

# Secret Service Agents

According to its Web site, the U.S. Secret Service has two missions. One is to protect the top-ranking governmental officials such as the president and vice president of the United States. Its other mission is to act as a law enforcement agency toward "safeguarding the payment and financial systems of the United States." This includes investigating the counterfeiting of U.S. currency. Given its dual focus of protection and criminal investigation, which mission of theirs would appear to be more dangerous than the other? Which area would offer more exciting jobs? If a person had a strong interest in money and finance, perhaps the financial and criminal aspect of the Secret Service may be more appealing. If a person were enthusiastic about the idea of working side by side with the president of the United States, that may be more interesting.

Secret Service agents don't only protect the president and vice president of the United States. Even Secretary of State Condoleeza Rice is escorted by Secret Service agents.

# Agents Who Protect

Do you think protecting the most powerful person in the world would be an exciting job for you? Imagine what it would be like to wake up knowing that your number-one mission for the day would be to keep the president of the United States safe and secure while he goes about his business of being president. While there hasn't been a successful attempt to hurt any of our presidents in twenty-five years, there may be a good reason for that. The U.S. Secret Service agency does everything it can to keep our nation's leaders safe.

A Secret Service agent is a highly competitive position that requires qualifications that only a few people hold. Consider what it would be like if, working for the Secret Service, you were responsible for making security arrangements for the president or vice president and their respective families to spend an evening at a small theater in New York City. You would have to coordinate with teams of agents on securing the entire building and investigate the backgrounds of those working for the production company putting on the show. You would also have to communicate with everyone throughout

U. S. COAST GUARD

the entire performance without interrupting the audience. Would you insist that metal detectors be on the premises? How many fellow team members would you think should work with you that night? Should you personally sit next to those that you are protecting during the performance? This is just one example of the extent to which a Secret Service agent may have to go in order to prevent conflict while our leaders are out in public.

# Agents Who Investigate

Do you know people who have had their personal information, like their Social Security number, financial records, or bank account numbers, used without their permission? Do you know if their information was successfully used for illegal purposes? Identity theft, the act of using another person's private information illegally, is one of the biggest challenges for the U.S. Secret Service today. With identity theft being a growing global problem, Secret Service agents are becoming more involved with the crime of funds taken from unsuspecting, law-abiding American citizens.

The pursuit of criminals who steal people's wallets and use their credit cards to buy goods and services is often left to local police departments. Major crimes where millions of financial accounts are accessed unbeknownst to their owners are usually handled by the Department of Homeland Security.

While customs agents generate revenues for the United States and its citizens by enforcing the payment of taxes and tariffs, the U.S. Secret Service attempts to protect citizens from losing their hard-earned money, as well as investigating those who commit financial crimes.

# What It Takes to Be a Homeland Security Officer

**2**

There are many different types of homeland security officers committed to the widespread mission of the Department of Homeland Security. Most of the more exciting occupations within the department, though, tend to require personality traits that are specifically related to these challenging jobs.

Both men and women are encouraged to apply for positions as homeland security officers if they have the education, experience, physical ability, talent, and character to get the job done and done well. More often than not, however, there aren't enough positions for everyone, so getting a homeland security office position can be highly competitive. There are many talented people out there, so the best way for a person to set himself apart and land a job within the department is to promote his own skills.

# Education

Based on the requirements of a job, many homeland security positions require a formal education, which often includes a specific or nonspecific college degree. Often, it also requires intensive training to prepare candidates for the work. A job candidate's education can include a four-year college degree, a two-year college degree, a two- or four-year technical college degree, or any combination of these types of formal educations. Additional training may even be obtained via one of the country's armed forces, such as the Army National Guard or United States Navy.

Some students may begin a college education focusing on one area of expertise. Halfway through their college experience, however, they may change their minds and decide to go down a completely different path. They may simply decide to develop and commit to totally different career goals.

For example, if a student begins her college education interested in becoming a doctor, what happens if she decides after her first year of college that medicine is

Students who consider working for the Department of Homeland Security can gain experience by first joining the armed forces.

no longer the career she wants to pursue? It's very likely that she could switch her educational focus to something new, which would normally force her to start all over. While medicine may have been her first choice after graduating from high school, business management may have been her second choice. The good thing about the Department of Homeland Security is that her degree in business would be a valuable asset to her candidacy should she ever want to apply for a position as a homeland security officer.

# Experience

Since the terrorist attacks on September 11, 2001, the national security industry has been one of the most popular areas of employment. While it's comforting to know that many educated people are interested in contributing to the country's protection by gaining employment within the Department of Homeland Security, a job as a homeland security officer often requires more than a good education and training. Another level of training not covered in the education criteria section of the department is something called on-the-job training.

On-the-job training relies heavily on the mental and physical experience of using the knowledge gained from technical training in real life. Image two recent college graduates applying for the same highly competitive position within the Department of Homeland Security. One has on-the-job training experience at a well-known government agency. The agency's hiring manager may value her candidacy over the other's due to her experience working in a similar role.

However, the hiring manager may find it difficult to choose if the other candidate has had experience as a volunteer firefighter or an emergency medical technician. Given that both candidates appear to have significant experience, perhaps they would both be invited in to begin the interview process. What if they are seen as equally qualified based on both education and experience? Additional criteria would be evaluated based on the needs of the job, such as physical ability.

# Physical Ability

How do you respond to exposure to extreme hot or cold temperatures? Of all of your friends, who do you

Similar to organizations like the U.S. Army, homeland security officer trainees have to be in shape to qualify to work for the organization.

think could withstand floating in a pool of water without any help the longest? If the job within the Homeland Security Department required someone who was a fast runner, such as a Secret Service agent, maybe a good candidate would be someone who was quick on her feet. If the position required someone who was very strong, a physically fit person could very well be the better team member.

The hiring manager may imagine a series of scenarios where physical demands on the team members would be at their greatest. Only then would a determination be made of which candidate would be better for the job. Some of the physical skills homeland security officers need to succeed in their occupations include high levels of energy, physical strength, and endurance.

# Talent

What are you really good at doing? Imagine you were competing against all your peers to be on the best team in the baseball or softball league in town. Who would be the best player? Would you consider yourself a top candidate?

People applying for jobs as homeland security officers often face the same style of rigorous competition. Pretend there are 100 candidates interested in getting a job offer for an exciting opportunity within the Department of Homeland Security. Imagine also that each and every one of them has the education, experience, and physical ability necessary to take on the demands of the job. How do you think the hiring manager would handle having too many skilled and eager candidates? He or she may consider an additional qualification, this time being talent or special skills.

By reviewing each and every candidate's profile, the manager would determine what special skills each candidate possessed. Of the 100, maybe 50 of them are fluent in more than one language. Of the 50 top candidates remaining, perhaps only 25 of those candidates have a pilot's license. Finally, of the final 25 people, maybe only 5 of those candidates have extensive experience in using firearms. One by one, each candidate would be crossed off the hiring manager's list, and in the end, only 3 would be considered to be the best candidates for the job compared to the other 97 people. There would then be one final evaluation to determine who would be offered the job.

# Character

Assuming that most jobs within the Department of Homeland Security require employees to work in some capacity on a team, it will be important for new team members to be well respected within the organization.

Leadership ability is a highly valued character trait among homeland security team members. People who are new to the organization need to be given strong direction.

Have any of your teachers asked you to work on a team with a few of your classmates in order to complete a group assignment? Why do you think it's important to not only enjoy working with other classmates on shared goals, but to work well with them, too? When it comes to fulfilling the requirements of highly stressful homeland security positions, character is usually the hardest because it is a trait that takes years to develop.

Hiring managers usually ask themselves, "Who is this person applying for this job? What are his or her true objectives in working with our organization? Is it to do good for our citizens and our country?" Judging from what the manager knows of the other team members, considerations would be made based on how well the new person transitions into the group. Other qualities of character, such as loyalty, honor, confidence, and one's commitment to upholding the law, would also be considered when evaluating a job candidate.

# Uniforms and Weapons

Y ou now have a few ideas of the types of exciting careers that are available and what it takes to obtain a job within them. As mentioned, people who have a specific level of education, experience, physical ability, talent, and character who want to work with the Department of Homeland Security face many challenges before even starting their jobs. This is due to the competitive nature of the job market. The more qualifications a job applicant has, the better off he or she will be when competing against hundreds of other people for one or two open positions.

Many of these jobs within the Department of Homeland Security entail wearing protective uniforms and using defensive weapons. Just as there are different agencies within the Department of Homeland Security, there are also different protective uniforms that homeland security officers in each division use, either on their day-to-day job or during special projects. For example, anyone who works for the U.S. Coast Guard is required to wear a life preserver.

The life preservers the Coast Guard uses are similar to ones you may have worn. Some U.S. Coast Guard life preservers are made to withstand a good deal of damage and include blinking lights that could be used to locate the person wearing it. Imagine what it would be like for a rescue swimmer working with the U.S. Coast Guard to jump into the ocean during a cold and dark night in order to save someone from drowning. Without the aid of the life preserver, the rescue swimmer would be unable to stay afloat for long periods of time and keep the head of the person whom he or she is attempting to rescue above water.

## Kevlar Vests

U.S. Secret Service agents sometimes wear vests, but they aren't used to survive in large bodies of water, like life preservers. Protective vests can be worn to shield an agent from the harm that assassins or terrorists may

Homeland security officers wear protective vests to keep them safe on the job. They take the highest precautions at all times, even while performing less dangerous missions.

attempt on high-profile government officials. If a Secret Service agent decided to wear a protective vest, it may be made of Kevlar, a flame-resistant and bullet-yielding fiber. In addition to protecting the body from harm, Kevlar protective vests also weigh less than other types of protective vests. Kevlar is also so versatile that it can be used to make other forms of protective gear such as boots, cut-resistant industrial gloves, and motorcycle helmets, as well as protective aprons, sleeves, and other types of clothing. While the three types of homeland security officers covered in this book may not use these additional Kevlar products, it is highly likely that other people within the department use them for their jobs.

The president of the United States is always surrounded by Secret Service agents dressed in dark suits and wearing sunglasses. If they are wearing protective vests, they would be worn underneath their dress shirts. Protective vests are thin enough to be concealed. Alternatively, however, customs agents may wear protective vests on the outside of their shirts or completely on top of their clothing. Whether they choose to conceal the protective vest depends on what type of image the homeland security officer wants to provide to the public.

Pretend that you're a customs agent walking around a dangerous city investigating criminal activities such as drug smuggling. You may wear regular clothing to look like an average civilian and a protective vest underneath your clothing to shield you from possible harm. Criminals are often less defensive when they are confronted by law enforcement agents who dress like ordinary citizens.

U. S. COAST

# Weapons

Homeland security officers may use many different types of tools in getting their jobs done right and in the safest manner possible. Secret Service agents, customs agents, and even Coast Guard officers sometimes have to resort to using protective weapons when dealing with criminals, especially to protect themselves while on the job.

## Firearms

Guns have been used for hundreds of years and are the most popular defensive weapon used by team members in the Department of Homeland Security out in the field. Coast Guard officers who board suspicious ships are always prepared for the unknown. What if they're attacked on board? What if a hostage situation takes place? By wearing firearms on their person, homeland security officers communicate a certain level of authority that is often helpful in preventing and dealing with possible conflict. However, while there are benefits to using this technology, there are also detriments.

While guns can save agents' lives, they can also be dangerous to the person using them for protection, such as in the event of the weapon getting into the hands of the enemy. For this reason, many homeland security officers, such as Coast Guard officers and customs agents, would rather resort to alternative means of protecting themselves than using guns, but sometimes it isn't possible due to certain situations. Secret Service agents, however, are inclined to use guns while protecting government officials and their families as well as themselves. They are required to stop assassins or terrorists from hurting anyone as soon as possible with as little chance for failure as possible.

## Mace and Pepper Spray

While firearms are a lethal way to prevent or stop criminals from hurting others, there are less-lethal protective weapons available to homeland security officers. Mace or pepper spray could be used if a Coast

Firearms training is important for homeland security officers. The Coast Guard, for example, is called upon to protect the ports of major cities such as New York during terror alerts.

Guard officer or customs agent is in close proximity to a criminal. These are tools that emit a liquid mix of chemicals that blind a person and cause temporary pain and discomfort if hit in the face with the spray. While these tools may be an alternative method of protecting oneself while on the job, the officer or agent would have to be very close, which in itself would be potentially dangerous. There may be a better solution, depending on the situation.

## Tasers

A company called Taser International invented a device, with the benefits of both a firearm and Mace, called a Taser. A Taser looks like a gun, but like Mace or pepper

Using a nonlethal weapon such as a Taser is often a safer solution than relying on a firearm.

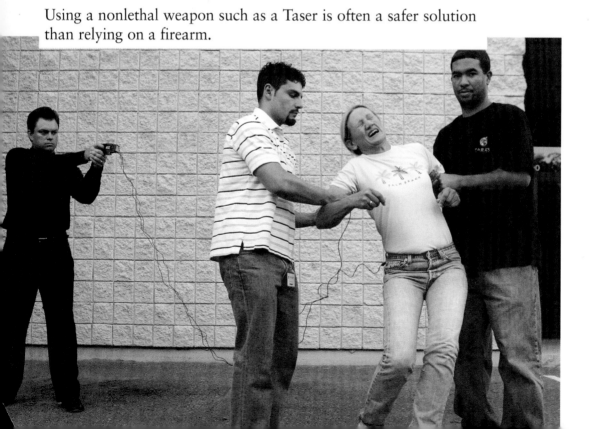

spray, it is used as a nonlethal weapon. Tasers, however, can be lethal when used improperly. It sends an electrical shock to the target's system for a short period of time.

In addition to looking and handling like a gun, Tasers can be used from distances greater than those needed to use a protective spray.

More and more law enforcement agencies within the United States are using Tasers as a complement to their firearms as they may be more appropriate in certain situations. Imagine you're a customs agent at an airport. You're searching someone who turns out to be one of the FBI's most wanted criminals. You know the person isn't carrying a firearm because you just searched him. To prevent immediate and possibly permanent bodily harm to the criminal, you may pull out your Taser instead of your gun to stop him from getting away before being taken into custody by police officers.

# Vehicles, Aircraft, and Watercraft

4

One of the exciting aspects of being a homeland security officer is using the equipment and rare modes of transportation to do successful work. People in other professions may travel via car or public transportation such as a bus or train. However, imagine what it would be like to go to work and spend the entire day in a vehicle created especially for your line of work. Do high-speed, high-tech methods of transportation interest you? One of the prerequisites of working as a homeland security officer such as a Coast Guard officer, customs agent, or Secret Service agent is having the interest in, being comfortable using, and being well-trained in working with unconventional tools to accomplish objectives on the job. It can be a lot of fun, too.

U. S. COAST

# By Land

After considering what it would be like to work in the air or in the water, homeland security officer positions that require candidates to work on solid ground rather than by sea or air may not seem exciting, but they can be. It all depends on the type of work the officer or agent is doing. Secret Service agents travel inside limousines or luxury cars that are made of protective armor and glass, which is often tinted. Have you ever seen news footage of the president and his staff arriving at a special event? Traditionally, there is a line of classy-looking, but well-protected, vehicles traveling from one place to another on streets that are closed off to the public until the fleet passes by the area. Inside those vehicles are Secret Service agents guarding America's government officials.

While the ride may feel comfortable psychologically, traveling in these vehicles can be a very stressful task. No one knows what lies in store for the agents should an assassin or terrorist be following or waiting for them at their destination. Customs agents travel in less classy vehicles. They may use SUVs, military jeeps, or even Humvees—

While it may look unusual for Secret Service agents to escort the president of the United States outside of the limousine, it helps to stop anyone from doing the president harm. The presidential limousine is also shielded with protective armor.

those large trucks that have similar characteristics to tanks. Humvees can travel at pretty high speeds given their weight, while carrying heavy equipment, protective vests, and defensive weapons.

# By Air

Homeland security officers also use airplanes and helicopters to protect America. Customs agents may use small airplanes to chase unyielding criminals in aircraft. Pretend that you're on a small jet with your team members, and your instrument panel inside the flight deck states that an unidentified flying object is 1,000 feet below you. Using techniques you learned during your training, you may follow the plane until you are able to identify it, call in the description to your headquarters, and determine if the people on board are criminals. The small jets can fly at very fast speeds over pretty far distances.

The HU-25 Guardian is no ordinary airplane. It can fly as high as 42,000 feet (12,800 meters) and as low as sea level. The HU-25 is a great aircraft for search and rescue missions, drug enforcement, and marine law enforcement operations.

Customs agents also use helicopters, which are more versatile. Whether helicopters are used depends on the needs during each operation, or mission. If agents want to access areas that would be impossible or dangerous for their fleet of planes to reach, then helicopters might be used. Similarly, Coast Guard officers can be trained to fly small planes and helicopters as well. While they may have similar duties to customs agents, Coast Guard officers use their helicopters to conduct search and rescue missions.

Do you like to swim? Imagine if you were a Coast Guard officer with the special duties of a rescue swimmer. Think about the exhilaration you would feel jumping out of a Coast Guard helicopter,

The HH-60 Jayhawk is the most recognized U.S. Coast Guard aircraft. It's a recovery helicopter that can't perform water landings, but can hover low to sea level.

landing in the ocean with a life preserver, and attempting to save a drowning, or unconscious, victim. According to its Web site, the U.S. Coast Guard uses five different types of aircraft, of which there are a little over 200 in use, including the HC-130 Hercules, HU-25 Guardian, HH-60 Jayhawk, HH-65A Dolphin, and MH-68A Stingray. Each of these aircraft has a different job.

The HH-65A Dolphin short-range recovery helicopter can hold four people, which includes two pilots, a flight engineer, and a rescue swimmer. On board are life preservers, communications and radar equipment, and a hoist unit that can lift up to 600 pounds.

Another example of one of the Coast Guard's aircraft is the MH-68A Stingray short-range armed interdiction helicopter, which traditionally has two pilots and one aviation gunner, a heavy caliber fire rifle, and a light caliber rifle, but is unable to perform water landings. The helicopter comes equipped with night vision, a forward looking infrared (FLIR) and visual video camera system, weather and ground mapping radar, an infrared searchlight, and a variety of communications equipment.

Secret Service agents, too, sometimes travel in helicopters and airplanes, including the well-known aircraft, Air Force One. Air Force One is the large airplane that is used to transport the president of the United States from one place to another over long distances. Depending on the assignment, a Secret Service agent may have the opportunity to work on that airplane if guarding the president.

# By Sea

When you think of a government organization that is associated with doing a significant amount of its work in the ocean, does the U.S. Coast Guard come to mind? While customs agents do use speedboats to track drug smugglers attempting to cross the country's borders, homeland security officers within the Coast Guard rely heavily on working in water. According to its Web site, the U.S. Coast Guard uses twenty-six "cutters" and seven types of boats. A cutter is a seagoing vessel that is sixty-five feet (20 meters) long or longer and provides accommodations for its crew to live inside. The seven types of boats that are used are forty-seven feet (14 meters) long or less and can include motor boats, utility boats, pursuit boats, and even inflatable boats. There

Coast Guard cutters are often the first vessels out to investigate conflicts on the water. They are almost unsinkable and can perform during the worst weather conditions at sea, such as hurricanes.

are around 1,400 of these boats in use.

Some people may not be good candidates for working as Coast Guard officers because they may be prone to seasickness. Think about the last time you were on a boat, big or small. If you enjoyed the experience and were excited by the speed of the vessel, you have one of the qualifications required for working as a Coast Guard officer: the ability to naturally adapt to the mobile experience out on the water. To some people, there is a strong sense of security working on land, but given the unique nature of working within the Coast Guard, there are many homeland security officers who enjoy their work because they understand the conditions of the job and welcome the challenges of working on, near, and often in, water.

Directly after New York City was attacked by terrorists on 9/11, the homeland security officers in the U.S. Coast Guard was on call to patrol the city's borders. They were looking to see if more attacks would be made and to communicate to other numerous law enforcement organizations the status of the devastated city from their perspective on the water.

Being a homeland security officer is a thrilling job. More important, however, the profession is admirable. There are few careers out there that allow you to protect and save lives on a daily basis. By working with a team of professionals that is dedicated to preserving the security of the United States, you can help make America a nation that continues to prosper for years to come.

# Glossary

**candidacy**  An application to an organization.

**character**  The quality of a person's personality or general behavior.

**detriment**  A specific disadvantage.

**devastated**  The state of being distressed.

**flight deck**  The area at the front of an airplane where the pilot is housed.

**identity theft**  The illegal or unethical misuse of another's personal information.

**Kevlar**  A type of material that is extremely strong and protective and is used in the manufacture of protective uniforms.

**lethal**  Something that is fatal.

**objective**  A goal or purpose.

**revenue**  Monetary income or proceeds.

**safeguard**  The act of protecting or ensuring safety.

**substance**  Any type of material or matter.

**suspect**  A person who is believed to be possibly guilty of a crime; the act of having such a belief about a person.

**suspicious**  The act of being doubtful or distrustful.

**SUV**  Sport utility vehicle.

**Taser**  A nonlethal defensive weapon that uses electricity to immobilize a target.

**tinted**  Colored or darkened; usually describes windows.

**unconventional**  The state of being different than the norm.

**versatile**  Having many purposes or uses.

**vessel**  A large ship or boat.

# For More Information

**Canadian Coast Guard**

Fisheries and Oceans Canada
  Communications Branch
200 Kent Street, 13th Floor, Station 13228
Ottawa, ON K1A 0E6
Canada
(613) 993-0999
Web site: http://www.ccg-gcc.gc.ca

**Canadian Security Intelligence Service**

National Headquarters
P.O. Box 9732 Station T
Ottawa, ON K1G 4G4
Canada
(613) 993-9620
Web site: http://www.csis-scrs.gc.ca

## U.S. Coast Guard

Coast Guard Headquarters
Commandant, U.S. Coast Guard
2100 Second Street SW
Washington, D.C. 20593
Web site: http://www.uscg.mil

## U.S. Customs and Border Protection

CBP Headquarters
1300 Pennsylvania Avenue NW
Washington, D.C. 20229
Web site: http://www.cbp.gov

## U.S. Department of Homeland Security

Washington, D.C. 20528
(202) 282-8000
Web site: http://www.dhs.gov/dhspublic

## U.S. Secret Service

Office of Government Liaison & Public Affairs
245 Murray Drive, Building 410
Washington, D.C. 20223
(202) 406-5708
Web site: http://www.ustreas.gov/usss

# Web Sites

Due to the changing nature of Internet links, Rosen Publishing has developed an online list of Web sites related to the subject of this book. This site is updated regularly. Please use this link to access the list:

http://www.rosenlinks.com/ec/hoso

# For Further Reading

Demarest, Chris L. *Mayday! Mayday! A Coast Guard Rescue*. New York, NY: Simon & Schuster Children's, 2004.

Evans, Fred. *Maritime and Port Security*. Philadelphia, PA: Chelsea House Publishers, 2004.

Keeter, Hunter. *The U.S. Homeland Security Forces*. Milwaukee, WI: Gareth Stevens Publishing, 2004.

Kerrigan, Michael. *The Department of Homeland Security*. Broomall, PA: Mason Crest Publishers, 2003.

Lyons, Lewis. *Rescue at Sea with the U.S. and Canadian Coast Guards*. Broomall, PA: Mason Crest Publishers, 2003.

Perl, Lila. *Terrorism*. New York, NY: Benchmark Books, 2004.

Schreiner, Samuel Agnew. *Mayday! Mayday! The Most Exciting Missions of Rescue, Interdiction, and*

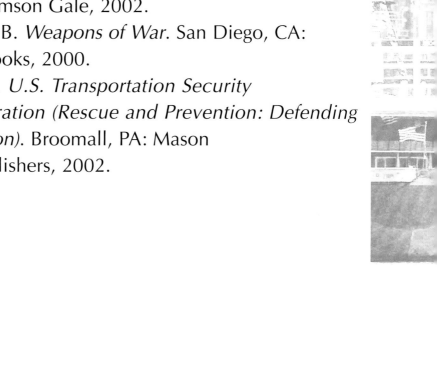

*Combat in the 200-Year Annals of the U.S. Coast Guard.* New York, NY: D.I. Fine, 1990.

Stewart, Gail B. *Defending the Borders: The Role of Border and Immigration Control.* San Diego, CA: Lucent Books, 2004.

Stewart, Gail B. *Terrorism.* San Diego, CA: Kidhaven Press/Thomson Gale, 2002.

Stewart, Gail B. *Weapons of War.* San Diego, CA: Lucent Books, 2000.

Wright, John. *U.S. Transportation Security Administration (Rescue and Prevention: Defending Our Nation).* Broomall, PA: Mason Crest Publishers, 2002.

# Bibliography

Dupont. "What Is Kevlar?" Retrieved January 30, 2006 (http://www.dupont.com/kevlar/whatiskevlar.html).

Floherty, John J. *Search and Rescue at Sea*. Philadelphia, PA: Lippincott, 1953.

Green, Michael. *Customs Service*. New York, NY: RiverFront Books, 1998.

Haulley, Fletcher. *This Is Your Government: The Department of Homeland Security*. New York, NY: Rosen Publishing Group, 2006.

Holden, Henry M. *Coast Guard Rescue and Patrol Aircraft*. Berkeley Heights, NJ: Enslow, 2002.

Innes, Brian. *International Terrorism*. Broomall, PA: Mason Crest Publishers, 2004.

Lord, Suzanne. *Drug Enforcement Agents*. New York, NY: Crestwood House, 1989.

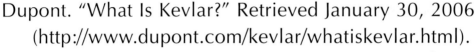

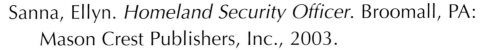

Sanna, Ellyn. *Homeland Security Officer*. Broomall, PA: Mason Crest Publishers, Inc., 2003.

United States Coast Guard. "Cutter, Aircraft, and Boat Datasheets." Retrieved March 13, 2006 (http://www.uscg.mil/datasheet/index.shtm).

United States Secret Service. "Investigative Mission." 2002. Retrieved January 30, 2006 (http://www. secretservice.gov/mission.shtml).

United States Secret Service. "Mission Statement." 2002. Retrieved January 30, 2006 (http://www. secretservice.gov/mission.shtml).

# Index

## About the Author

Jared Meyer is an author and educator who works with students on improving their decision-making and communication skills. He has authored several books on both developing critical-thinking skills and college and career exploration for young readers. Meyer works with Monster Worldwide's Making It Count programs and speaks with large groups of high school students on making personal choices about their college search, college experience, and career. He may be contacted at jaredmeyer@makstar.com.

## Photo Credits